Pizza for Pia

By
Betsy Groban

Illustrated by
Allison Steinfeld

Ready-to-Read

Simon Spotlight
New York   London   Toronto   Sydney   New Delhi

For Pia. This one's for you, with love from G-Ma. —B. G.

For Marathon Mike. Thank you for always helping me cross the finish line. —A. S.

SIMON SPOTLIGHT

An imprint of Simon & Schuster Children's Publishing Division
1230 Avenue of the Americas, New York, New York 10020
This Simon Spotlight edition May 2024 · Text copyright © 2024
by Betsy Groban · Illustrations copyright © 2024 by Allison Steinfeld
All rights reserved, including the right of reproduction in whole or in part
in any form. · SIMON SPOTLIGHT, READY-TO-READ, and colophon are
registered trademarks of Simon & Schuster, LLC · Simon & Schuster:
Celebrating 100 Years of Publishing in 2024 · For information about special
discounts for bulk purchases, please contact Simon & Schuster Special
Sales at 1-866-506-1949 or business@simonandschuster.com. The Simon &
Schuster Speakers Bureau can bring authors to your live event. For more
information or to book an event contact the Simon & Schuster Speakers
Bureau at 1-866-248-3049 or visit our website at www.simonspeakers.com.
Manufactured in the United States of America 0324 LAK
2 4 6 8 10 9 7 5 3 1
Library of Congress Cataloging-in-Publication Data · Names: Groban,
Betsy, author. | Steinfeld, Allison, illustrator. · Title: Pizza for Pia / by Betsy
Groban ; illustrated by Allison Steinfeld. · Description: Simon Spotlight
edition. | New York : Simon Spotlight, 2024. | Series: Ready-to-read.
Level 1 | Audience: Ages 4 to 6. | Summary: Pia bravely informs her pizza-
loving family that she wants something different to eat. · Identifiers: LCCN
2023029912 (print) | LCCN 2023029913 (ebook) | ISBN 9781665947008
(paperback) | ISBN 9781665947015 (hardcover) | ISBN 9781665947022
(ebook) · Subjects: CYAC: Pizza—Fiction. | Family life—Fiction.
LCGFT: Picture books. | Readers (Publications)
Classification: LCC PZ7.1.G759 Pi 2024 (print) | LCC PZ7.1.G759 (ebook)
DDC [E]—dc23 · LC record available at https://lccn.loc.gov/2023029912
LC ebook record available at https://lccn.loc.gov/2023029913

Pia loves to eat.

"Mealtime is the best time," says Pia.

Pia loves pizza.

That is what her family says.

"I will make the pizza," says Pia's pop, Pete.

"Please add peppers," says Pia's mom, Penny.

"I only like cheese
on my pizza,"
says Pia's cousin, Pedro.

"I can put peppers on half," says Pia's pop. "That is easy."

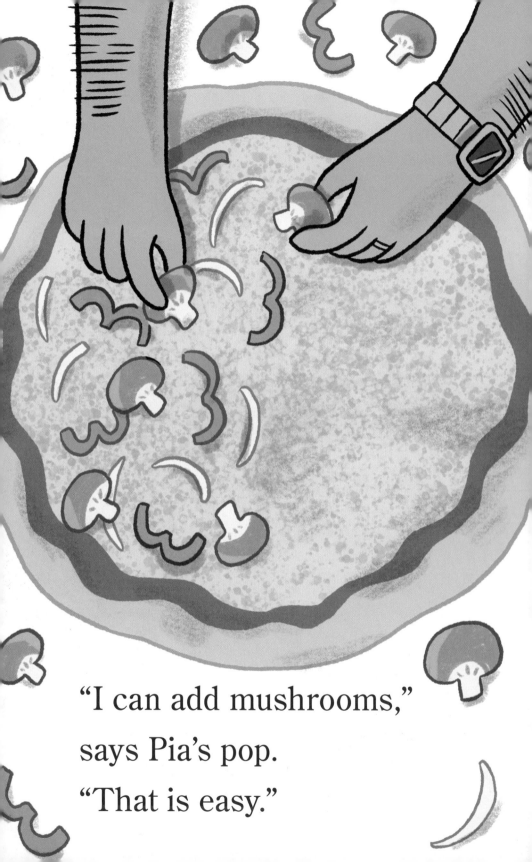

"I can add mushrooms,"
says Pia's pop.
"That is easy."

"What do you want on your pizza, Pia?" asks Pia's pop.

"I do not like pizza,"
whispers Pia.

What did Pia say?

But we all love pizza.

"Not me," says Pia.
"I want TACOS!"

Pia's family has an idea.

They warm up taco shells in the oven.

They add mushrooms.

They add peppers.

They add cheese.

They add onions.

HOORAY, TACOS FOR PIA!